ELLA

Diaries

TOP SECRET!

With special thanks to Jaime-Anna and
Abbey, and the Gold St PS reading club:
Chloe, Kitty, Esther, Claire, Sabine, Alicia,
Zach, Eugenie, Lara, Lucy and Robert—M.C.

Meredith Costain

For everyone who is scared
of horses—like me!—D.M.

Danielle M°Donald

First American Edition 2016
Kane Miller, A Division of EDC Publishing

Text copyright © Meredith Costain, 2016
Illustrations copyright © Danielle McDonald, 2016

First published by Scholastic Australia, a division of Scholastic Australia Pty Limited in
2016. This edition published under license from Scholastic Australia Pty Limited.

Library of Congress Control Number: 2015954199

Printed and bound in the United States of America

5 6 7 8 9 10

ISBN: 978-1-61067-524-6

ELLA

Diaries

Pony School
Showdown

Kane Miller
A DIVISION OF EDC PUBLISHING

Thursday, after school

Dear Diary,

Guess what? You know how my best friend Zoe is HORSE MAD? Well, there's a special word for that.

Hippophile.

A hippophile is someone who is CRAZY about horses. Just like Zoe!

It's driving ME crazy!

She talks about horses all the time! She knows all the different types, like Shetland ponies and quarter horses and draft horses.

And the different designs you can get them in, like spotty and not spotty.

And what they eat (carrots and grass) and don't eat (fish sticks).

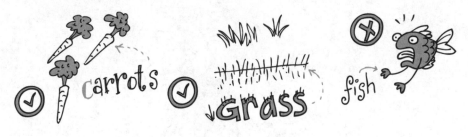

Zoe goes to Pony School every week, where she learns even MORE STUFF about horses.

STUFF ZOE LEARNS AT PONY SCHOOL

* How to get on and off a horse gracefully.

* How to braid their manes and tails.

bangs

Braided **Tail**

Braided **mane BOWS**

* How to ride them around and around in a circle without falling off.

And she is always telling me interesting horsey facts like:

Zoe's Horsey Fact #1: Horses can sleep when they are lying down AND standing up.

Zoe's Horsey Fact #2: Baby horses can stand up only an hour after they are born. Wow!

Zoe's Horsey Fact #3: Horses' hoofs are actually gigantic toenails. Eww. Imagine having toenails that big!

And these are only *three* of the ~~210~~ ~~356~~ ~~389~~ 439 different facts that Zoe knows about horses. Which is ~~210~~ ~~356~~ ~~389~~ ~~439~~ more facts than I know. Mainly because I don't spend my every waking hour thinking about or reading about or drawing horses like Zoe does.

THINGS I KNOW ABOUT HORSES

① They have four legs and a swishy tail.

② They make strange noises with strange names, like "whinny."✳

3 There are lots of books and movies about them. The horses always have names like Misty or Moonlight and the girls that ride them are called Arabella or Jill.

Arabella   Jill

4 It is a loooooong way to the ground if you fall off them.

✻ Zoe's Horsey Fact #4: Whinny is the "whe-e-e-e-e-e-e-e!" sound horses make when they are happy or excited to see you. They also nicker, snort and neigh.

Zoe is CONSTANTLY telling me that horses are HER LIFE, and if I was a true best friend I would make them MY LIFE as well. Which isn't very fair because, as everyone knows, my life is all about fabulously fabulous things like poetry and songwriting, and gymnastics, and ballet, and fashion, and being super stylish.

I think it would be very hard to be fashionable and super stylish if you were bumping around on the back of a large sweaty animal all day long, worrying about being thrown into a muddy ditch.

But I said I would at least think about it,
because that is what BFFs do.

See you later, Diary,
Ella
XOXO

Friday night, before bed

Dear Diary,

Tonight was Mom and Dad's wedding anniversary. Dad gave Mom a gigantic bunch of red roses and a big sloppy kiss, IN FRONT OF EVERYONE. Eww. It was sooo emBARRassing. Then they went out for dinner to a fancy restaurant.

Mom

Dad

Gigantic RED ROSES

I had told Mom and Dad not to worry about getting a babysitter because I could look after Max and Olivia all by myself and would make sure they brushed their teeth properly (front and back) and went to bed on time.

This is what I was going to make us all for dinner:

Main course: Family-size pizza with everything (from Papa Peppino's Pizza delivery service).

Pizza
with everything!

~~Desert~~ Dessert: Banana splits with double extra ~~hazelnut~~ hazelnut fudge ice cream and triple extra chocolate syrup (with optional crushed nuts and chocolate and/or strawberry sprinkles).

And then, after Max and Olivia went to bed and I superglued their doors shut so they couldn't come back out to the family room and annoy me, I was going to stay up really late, sitting on the sofa with Bob eating caramel popcorn and watching *So You Think You Can Be a Style Queen* on TV.

SO YOU THINK YOU CAN BE A *Style* QUEEN

But Mom said, "Thank you very much for offering, Ella, but Nanna Kate is coming over to look after you all," which made me feel like a BIG BABY. And then I remembered Nanna Kate is ~~acksh~~ actually a really fun babysitter, especially when she helps me put together stylish outfits.

~~unforch~~ Unfortunately Nanna Kate is on "a health kick," so instead of yummy pizza and banana splits for dinner we had vegetable stacks with double broccoli (bleuchhh) and stewed plums with creamed rice (double bleuchhh).

DOUBLE ?⁓⁓ Broccoli

zucchini

Peas

CARROT

Mashed potato

VEGGIE STACK

Bleuchhh!

DOUBLE

Bleuchhh!

Stewed PLUMS

creamed RICE

And then Nanna Kate said if we brushed our teeth and got into our jim-jams superfast she'd let us all stay up and watch a very special program on TV that she knew we would all LOVE.

And I got really excited and said, "Ooooo, do you mean that fabulously fabulous show about being a style queen?" But sadly she didn't, so I didn't get to watch it after all. ☹

Sigh.

But guess what? The TV show we did watch was all about these beautiful white horses called ~~Lipper~~ Lipizzaners. And they were rearing up on their back legs and waving their front legs in the air, and leaping and jumping doing these fancy steps called caprioles, with their legs sticking out at the back like ballet dancers. It was aMAZing! They must have done heaps of practicing, just like I do in gymnastics and ballet.

capriole

And the riders were all wearing super-stylish, tight-fitting jackets and riding boots that went all the way up to their knees! They were the best, most stylish boots I HAVE EVER SEEN!

Best
Riding BOOTS

I wonder if Zoe gets to wear boots like that when she goes to Pony School?

Good night, Diary.
xOxO

Saturday morning, after breakfast

Good morning, Diary,

Mom and Dad are going shopping for a special anniversary gift today so Nanna Kate is taking Olivia and Max and me to the circus.

I hope they have horses there. I CAN'T STOP thinking about the Lipper-whatsy horses I saw on the TV show last night. They were so graceful and elegant and fashionable. (Hmmm . . . now who does THAT remind you of . . . ☺)

ME

Graceful

FASHIONABLE Elegant

Talk soon!
E

Saturday night, before bed

Dearest Diary,

The circus was aMAzing!

We saw clowns and fire-eaters and fire-eating clowns and tightrope walkers spinning plates on their noses.

CLOWNS

spinning PLATE

Tightrope walker

And guess what? They DID have horses!

A girl wearing a really sparkly outfit with feathers in her hair came out. Her name was Rosa and she had a beautiful white horse called Star. She jumped up onto Star and stood on his back. Then she rode around doing fancy moves in time to the music.

ROSA

Star

She even did a backflip on top of him—just like I do on the balance beam at Twisters!

Zow-ee! I never knew that horses were so artistic! You can do tricks and ballet and gymnastic moves and wear super-stylish sparkly outfits with feathers and ride a horse all at the same time! All the things I LOVE!

That's it. I am DEFINITELY getting a horse. I can't wait till the morning so I can tell Zoe!

Good night, Diary.
Sweet dreams.
Love, Ella

Sunday, just before lunch

Dear Diary,

As soon as I woke up, I called Zoe and arranged to have an EMERGENCY MEETING at her place right after breakfast.

ME

ZOE

Zoe's bedroom is the PERFECT PLACE to have an Emergency Meeting about horses because it looks just like the inside of a horse shed.

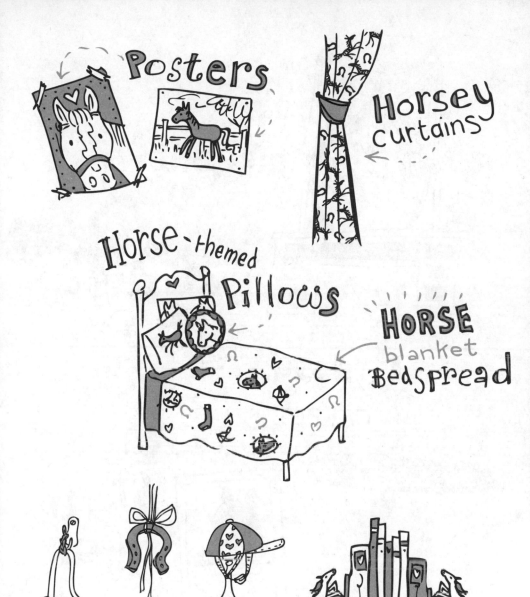

Posters

Horsey curtains

Horse-themed Pillows

HORSE blanket Bedspread

HORSE-themed Decorations

Rosettes
AND
RiBBONS

TOY
HORSE
·COLLECTION·

Grassy
CARPET

Fake
STABLE
DOOR
sticker

Zoe shoved a heap of toy horses off her bed onto the floor to make enough room for us both to sit down. When we were comfy I told her all about the Lipper-whatsy horses and their beautiful ballet dancing and Rosa and the backflip she did on Star's back. And how I was sorry I hadn't paid enough attention when she'd told me how amazing and excellent horses are, but now I was ready to make them MY life as well, not just because that's what BFFs do, but because I absolutely, completely, sincerely, GENUINELY believed it.

And then I said if I didn't get a horse
IMMEDIATELY I would DIE.

Zoe looked a bit shocked. But then she
made this sound that was exactly like a
horse whinnying. (You know, that sound
horses make when they are
happy or excited to see you.)

Whinny

And then Zoe said, "This is so
amazing because there is a spare spot at
my Pony School right now because Arabella
Smythe dropped out. As soon as you get
your horse you can start coming with me
so you can learn how to ride it! It is going
to be FABULOUS!"

And I said, "Zoe, you are BRILLIANT!!!"

And Zoe said, "I KNOW!!!"

It was SO EXCITING!

And then we spent the rest of our Emergency
Meeting talking about:
Ⓐ where I was going to keep my new horse✳
Ⓑ what I was going to feed it✳✳
Ⓒ what I was going to call it✳✳✳

✳ In our backyard.
✳✳ Grass and carrots.

GRASS

carrots

OUR Backyard

*** This one took up the most time. Here are some of the exciting names we came up with:

ME	ZOE
Star	Blaze
Hurricane	Gypsy
Lightning	Honey
Luna	Blossom
Destiny	~~Misty~~
Bandit	Amber
Lord Danger	Buttercup
Comet	~~Moonlight~~

There are already too many other horses called this.

Now all I have to do is convince Mom and Dad to let me get one. ~~Forch~~ Fortunately I have a BRILLIANT PLAN so it will be easy-peasy.

I CAN'T WAIT!!!

Sunday, after lunch

Dear ~~Dairy~~ Diary,

I can't believe it. Mom and Dad said no!

WAAAAAAAAHHHHHHHH!

This is what happened:

Me (whistling): Wh wh wh wh wh wh wh whhhh wwwh . . .

Olivia (whiny voice): Stop that, Ella, you're making my brain hurt.

Dad: You sound very cheery today, Ella.

Me (cheerily): That's because I am. I'm so lucky to have such a lovely, kind,

sweet, adorable, loving family. Especially you, Mom and Dad.

Mom (nervously): You haven't broken anything, have you?

Me (shocked): No, of course not! Why would you even think that?

Mom (sighing): Never mind.

Me (casually): Have you looked out the window lately?

Mom (suspiciously): Why? What's out there? Is Bob digging holes in the garden again?

Me: No. Bob's under the table, eating Olivia's broccoli.

Olivia: Ell-aaa! He IS NOT!

Max (pointing under the table): Yes, he is. I sawed him! He's eating Dadda's broccoli too.

Dad (looking guilty): Nonsense. Don't make up silly stories, Max. (Changing the subject quickly.) So tell us, Ella. What *is* outside the window?

Me (sweetly): Grass.

Mom: Grass?

Me: Grass. Have you noticed how long it's getting?

Dad: Er . . . no?

Me (seriously): Well, it is. REALLY, REALLY long. Way too long for you to mow with the lawn mower, Dad. It would probably get stuck in the engine part and whizz around and around until it broke into a gazillion pieces. And then the grass would grow and grow and keep on growing until it was so long we wouldn't be able to see out of the window at all. We would be trapped in here in the darkest dark, bumping into each other all the time. But never fear. I have the PERFECT SOLUTION!

Mom (suspiciously): And what's that?

Me (cunningly): A horse! If we had a horse, it could eat all that long grass for you. And you wouldn't ever have to mow it again! Think of all A Horse! the spare time you'd have left over to do all your favorite things!

Mom and Dad (together):

NOOOO∘∘…

Mom

Dad

Me (desperately): But it's my birthday next week! Pl-e-e-e-e-e-e-ase can I have a horse?

And then Mom and Dad told me all the reasons why I can't have a horse. Even a really small cute one that didn't eat much. ☹

REASONS WHY I CAN'T HAVE A HORSE

① It costs gigantic amounts of money to feed and look after them and we can't afford it.

2 It is against the
law to keep horses
in your backyard.

3 And even if you could, they would eat
all the plants and the laundry on the
line and leave gigantic piles of stinky horse
poop everywhere.

Yum!
Yum!

Stinky
HORSE
POOP
(Eww!)

4 The neighbors would complain about the smell from all the horse poop. (Eww.) And the flies hanging around the horse poop. (Double eww.) And also the whinnying every time I went outside and it was happy or excited to see me.

Whinny

5 It might step on Bob.

POOR BOB

6 There wouldn't be enough room for it to run around and it might get sick.

~~unforch~~ unfortunately, these are all VERY
GOOD reasons. (Especially the one about
stepping on Bob, who is too lazy and fat
from eating everyone's broccoli to get out
of the way.) So even if I promised to clean
my room every day in a row for 900
trillion gazillion years, I STILL wouldn't get
Mom and Dad to change their mind.

Fat Bob

After lunch I called Zoe to see if she had
any ideas for me. Zoe ALWAYS has
exceptionally excellent ideas.

ME

ZOE

She didn't. ☹

It's SO NOT FAIR, Diary! I have to have a horse. I just HAVE to.

I need to think up another plan.

Yours in desperate desperation,
Ella

Sunday night, very, very, very late

Dear Diary,

I have been lying here for HOURS trying to think up another plan, but all my ideas so far are hopelessly hopeless. ☹

So I wrote this shape poem about horses instead.

Horses
are amazing.
They are
graceful and
free-spirited,
powerful and
strong, like
a poem or
a song.
Horses run around the
paddock kicking up their heels,
and they prance and they dance with
their swishing tails held high in the air.
Horses have gleaming coats and soulful
eyes. They walk and trot and canter
and gallop, running free like the
wind. If I had a horse I would
love it always and forever.
And I would call it STAR.

walk	walk
walk	walk
walk	walk
walk	walk
trot	trot
trot	trot
trot	trot
gallop	gallop
canter	canter

I'm going to make hundreds of copies of my poem and put them all over the house where Mom and Dad won't be able to miss them.* And then they will be able to see just how SERIOUSLY SERIOUS I am about getting a horse of my very own.

* Like on the coffee machine and the bathroom mirror and Mom's computer screen and the back of the bathroom door and inside the cookie jar and in the shower and across the car

coffee MACHINE

(poem)

MoM's computer SCREEN

windshield and on their pillows and in their bed. Ha-ha, there will be NO ESCAPE!!! ☺

All this poem writing is very hard work, Diary. Just as well it is school vacation tomorrow, I will be able to sleep in.

Good night, Diary Doo.
Thanks for always being there for me.
Ella x

Monday morning, I'm not exactly sure of the time, but way too early for someone who was awake half the night writing parent-persuading poems

I was right in the middle of a fabulous dream about riding a beautiful white horse wearing a sparkly tutu (me,  not the horse) when Olivia screeched, "Ella, phone call for you!" really loudly in my ear and dropped the phone on my bed, and the dream went Pffffftttttt! and disappeared, just like that. And so did my beautiful white horse and sparkly tutu. ☹

Thanks, O-LIV-ia.

It was Zoe. She wants me to come over for an emergency Emergency Meeting at her house IMMEDIATELY.

Ooooo. I wonder what she wants? This is seriously EXCITING!

Speak soon, Diary!

Monday, a bit later that morning

You are NEVER going to believe what happened just now, so I'll tell you anyway.

After Zoe's phone call, I rushed straight over to her house and we moved all her toy horses off her bed again so we could have our meeting.

This is what we said.

Zoe (her eyes all shiny
like a horse's coat
sparkling in the sparkly
sunshine after it has
been shampooed and brushed with a special
horse-brushing brush): I told Mom all about
how you desperately want to make horses
YOUR LIFE just like me, only you're not
~~aloud~~ allowed and guess what?
Me: Your mom is going to adopt me and
buy me a horse for my
birthday?
Zoe: Nope. Guess again.
Me: You and I are
going to run away to
the circus and become

internationally famous bareback-riding circus stars?

Zoe: Nope. Guess again.

Me: I give up. Just tell me.

So Zoe said her mom, who is the accountant✱ for Zoe's Pony School, had a BRILLIANT IDEA! Pony School is going to be open every day for the next two weeks because it's school vacation. And I could rent a horse just like Zoe does and go with her. She said her mom could even get me a special discount. But the best thing is she said she would talk to *my* mom and dad about why it would be good for me to go to Pony School with Zoe.

✳ An accountant is NOT a special type of ant that is good at counting. That 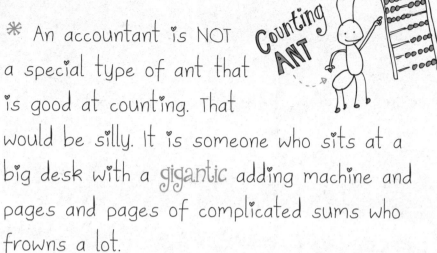 would be silly. It is someone who sits at a big desk with a gigantic adding machine and pages and pages of complicated sums who frowns a lot.

Zow-ee! Zoe's mom is like my own personal Fairy Godmother. ☺☺☺

As soon as I got home I told Mom about what Zoe's mom said and to expect an important call ANY MOMENT from her. And Mom said, "Hmmm" and, "I'll have to discuss it all with Dad" and, "We'll see."

That sounds really hopeful . . . doesn't it?

Now I just need to find something to wear!

E x

Monday night, before dinner

Waiting ~~paysh~~ patiently for
Mom or Dad to say something
about me going to Pony School.

Nothing so far. Maybe Zoe's mom hasn't
called them yet?

Monday night, after dinner

Still nothing. Even though I ate ALL my broccoli and let Olivia borrow my best mauve gel pen and cleared the table without being asked, to prove how kind and ~~responsabubble~~ responsible I am.

I also did a few quiet whinnies as a gentle reminder of how much I need horses in my life, but I'm not 100% sure if my cold and uncaring family even noticed them.

Whinny!

I am desperately and deeply ~~distrort~~ distraught, dear Diary. Maybe I should run away and join the circus after all?

Tuesday morning

Still nothing.

School vacation is BORING. Here is a list of the things I have done so far:

It is so not fair. If I was at Pony School Vacation Club with Zoe, I could be doing ZILLIONS of things and having fun, fun, fun!

Tuesday, before lunch

Still nothing.

All this waiting is making me go a bit twitchy, Diary. Do you think I should spread around some more copies of my shape poem, in case Mom and Dad missed the first ones?

Tuesday night

Dearest, darlingest Diary,

It's all arranged! Zoe's mom spoke to my mom and my mom said yes and I'm going to start going to Vacation Club at Zoe's Pony School TOMORROW!!!

Zoe and I spent all afternoon putting together my Pony School outfit. I wanted to wear a sparkly tutu with feathers in my hair like Rosa from the circus, but Zoe said everyone else just wore plain, sensible

Sparkly Tutu
NO

Feathers IN MY HAIR
NO

things like stretchy ~~jodpers~~ jodhpurs and polo shirts. (Bleuchhh. So boring.)
She is lending me an old pair of her joddies* and her mom's riding helmet until I can get my own.

POLO SHIRT

Jodhpurs
(Joddies)

HELMET

* Zoe says "joddies" is what all the cool girls at Pony School call their jodhpurs, so I will too.

I wanted to wear my second-best tiara (rather than my first-best one, in case it fell off and a horse stood on it), but Zoe says you have to wear a helmet in case you fall off your horse and hit your head and all your  brains fall out. So I'm going to wear the helmet AND my tiara. I want to look EXTRA SPECIAL on my first official day as a horse lover.

After Zoe went home, I added some extra stylish features to my outfit using sparkly glitter and a tube of strong glue✳✳ I borrowed from Dad's workshop. It looks aMAZing.

** ~~unforch~~ Unfortunately some of the strong glue spilled on Bob and then he accidentally bumped into the table where I put the glitter, so he has been glitterized as well. He looks BEAUTIful. ☺
I CAN'T WAIT until tomorrow!

BOB

Glitterized Patches

Bye for now,
Ella xx

Wednesday night, before dinner

Dear Diary,

There is just so much to tell you!

As soon as we got to Pony School I ran straight over to the first horses I saw to make sure I got the best one.

They were all just standing there in a yard flicking their tails and stamping their hoofs and tossing their heads and making snorty sounds out of their gigantic noses.

And then a girl with white joddies came out

of the horse shed and said, "Ex-cuuuuuse me? Can I help you?" and I pointed to a big white horse that looked a bit like Star from the circus and said, "Yes, please. I'll have that one."

And then the girl said, "Oh really?" with this big smirky smirk all over her face.

Big
SMIRKY
Smirk

And I said, "Yes, it looks amazing. I can't wait to ride it." I reached over the rail and gave it a little pat on its neck part. And then the horse did a big whinny and stood up on its back legs and waved its front hoofs around in the air, just like the Lipper-whatsy horses on the TV show.

Then another girl with a yellow ponytail and long black riding boots up to her

PAT ON THE Neck Part

ME

Whinny!

knees came running out of the horse shed and screeched, "Hey, you! Get away from my horse!"

Then she started stroking its side part and saying calming-down things like, "There, there, Misty," and, "My darling widdle precious babykins sweetie pie, did that nasty girl scare you?"

After about nine hours of being stroked,
the horse stopped whinnying and standing
up on its back legs and
just stood there glaring
glaringly at me.

Glaring
Glaringly

And then the first
girl said in this really
snooty voice, "Tiara Girl thinks she can
ride your horse." And then the second girl
looked me up and down and said in an even
snootier voice, "Ha! Little Miss Glitter looks
like she couldn't even ride a rocking horse."
And then they both threw their heads back
and laughed a really nasty-pasty laugh.

Like this:

I was just about to tell them they could keep their silly horse, I didn't like it anyway, when I saw Zoe waving at me like a crazed chicken. She was up at the other end of the horse yard with all the other Pony School girls.

ZOE

Then she did this complicated series of
secret hand signals to let me know I was in
the wrong place and to come up to her end
IMMEDIATELY.

I sent an even more complicated series of
secret hand signals back to say thanks for
telling me, how was I supposed to know
where to go and now I'm going to look really
silly. ☹

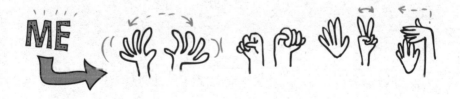

Then I casually strolled over to the right place, like I knew EXACTLY what I was doing the whole time, even though on the inside I was desperately distraught. Then I bravely told Zoe what the snooty girls said to me.

She was SHOCKED.

SHOCKED

This is what we said next.
Zoe: I am SHOCKED.
Me: Same.
Zoe: Anyone with even a tiny brain would know you were new and don't know anything yet. It's not your fault you did something really silly.

Me (wiping away a silent tear. Now even Zoe, who is *supposed to be* my BFF, thinks I'm silly): Maybe I should just go home. I am hopeless at horses.

Zoe (putting her arm around me and giving me nice calming-down pats): Don't worry, Letitia and Lavinia think they are better than everyone else because they have their own horses and we don't, but they're not. They're just mean old nasty-pasties.

Then she told me there are two types of horses at Pony School:

1 Horses that belong to their owners.

"Owner" ★ Horse

2 Horses that belong to Pony School.

PONY **SCHOOL** ♥ *horse*

And that I must NEVER EVER try to ride an owned horse. ESPECIALLY if it is Lavinia's or Letitia's.

Lavinia

And then just when I was thinking the day couldn't get any worse, something much, MUCH worse than that happened. You'll never guess wh

Letitia

Sorry, Diary. Have to go. Dad's calling me for dinner! I'll tell you what happened when I get back.

E xx

Wednesday night, straight after dinner

I'm back! Sorry I took so long but Mom and Dad and Max and Olivia wanted to know EVERYTHING about my day. Like:

♥ what we did at Pony School and
☆ if I'd made any new friends and
🦋 if my pony was nice and
🐾 what its name was.

So anyway, after my BIG MISTAKE I started looking at the Pony School horses instead. I'd just picked out a really nice-looking yellow one with a white tail and stylish superlong eyelashes when a big silver car drove through the gates. And then a girl wearing white and gold EVERYTHING climbed out of it.

YELLOW HORSE

White TAIL

Stylish superlong EyeLashes

White Hair TiE

White POLO SHIRT

White wrist BANDS

GOLD Riding HELMET

White JoddiES

Gold KNEE-length Riding BOOTS

And guess who it was?

Precious Princess

Peach Parker is the most annoying girl in the history of annoying girls. Not only that, she always has to copy everything I do. It's SO NOT FAIR! Coming to Pony School was MY idea! Well actually it was Zoe's, but since we're BFFs, that's practically the same thing.

I was hoping Princess Peach would make the same BIG MISTAKE as me. But she came straight over to our group and just stood there with this really bored I-am-so-much-better-than-you look on her face. The same look Letitia had when she said I couldn't even ride a rocking horse.

Ha! Maybe Letitia is Peach's evil twin sister from another dimension!

I-am-so-much-BETTER-than-YOU

PEACH
Looking
BORED

Then a lady called June
came out of our horse
shed to ask everyone
which horse or pony we'd
like today. I was just
about to tell her I'd like
the pretty yellow one,
please, when Peach pushed
in front of me and said

♧JUNE♧

in her sucky, whiny, teacher's
pet voice, "Ooooooo, look at
that DARLING palomino.✽ It
matches my outfit EXACTLY. I
just HAVE to have that one."

And then she did a little twirl
so we all could see her white
and gold riding outfit AGAIN.

And June said, "Yes, of course,
you MUST have Blondie, she's
absolutely PERFECT
for you," and handed
her Blondie's lead rope.
Grrrrrrrrr.
How DARE Peach steal
MY horse!!!

White Mane

White Tail

GOLDEN COAT

Palomino HORSE

* Zoe's Horsey Fact #5: Palominos are a
type of horse. They have a golden coat and
a white mane and tail.

Zoe gave me another calming-down pat and said, "Don't worry, there are lots of other really nice ponies here." And then she asked June if we could have Snowy and Patches.

Snowy and Patches are very nice, friendly horses with pattable neck parts. Snowy is white✳✳ with a fluffy coat just like a teddy bear. And Patches is white with brown patches. They are Best Friends, just like Zoe and me. ☺

ZOE

ME

♥ Best Friends

** Zoe's Horsey Fact #6: white horses
are called grays, even though they are ~~acksh~~
actually white. (whoever thought that up
must have a REALLY strange brain.)

And horses that have black and white
splodges everywhere are called piebald. Which
is just WEIRD.

June told us all to take our horses into the horse shed so we could "tack up." Tacking up is a special horsey word that means putting the saddle and bridle bits on your horse so you can ride it. I was just about to tell June I didn't need to tack anything up because I was going to ride Patches bareback like the lady in the circus, when nasty-pasty Letitia and Lavinia trotted over grandly on their grand and sleek owned horses.

SADDLE

SEAT

Stirrup

Bit

Reins

BRidLE

And guess what?
Letitia looked straight
at Peach and said,
"Hello, Peachy-Pie, what
are YOU doing here?"
in this really posh,
hoity-toity voice.

Peach's face went dark, like a black thunder
cloud had just passed across the sunny
sun. Scary lightning bolts shot
out of her eyes.

Peach stood there glaring at Letitia for about 900 hours. Then she stormed off with her nose in the air.

Zoe and I exchanged MEANINGFUL LOOKS. Then we took Snowy and Patches into the horse shed so we could tack them up.

Tacking up is REALLY HARD. There are so many things to remember, like tying your pony up first so he doesn't wander off to the other side of the horse shed when you're not looking. ☹

Once I got Patches to come back, I brushed him all over with a special grooming brush which he LOVED. Then I put the saddle on his back. Then I took the saddle OFF his back and put it on again so it was facing the right way. ☺

Then there was a really hard bit where I had to put the bit bit in Patches' mouth part without him biting my finger off (OUCH!) and the bridle bit over his ear parts. And then FINALLY Patches was ready to ride. YAY!

This part was REALLY Confusing!

I've got so much more to write about my first day at Pony School, Diary, but Mom says if I don't turn the light off and go to sleep IMMEDIATELY, I will be too tired to go back to Pony School tomorrow.

I CAN'T WAIT!!!
Good night.
Love,
Ella xOxO

Wednesday night, very, very late

Dearest Diary,

I have been lying here for hours desperately trying to get comfy but something must be wrong with my bed. Every time I lie down it makes different parts of me hurt.

Parts of ME that hurt

SIDE VIEW

My Back

MY Bottom

The BACK OF MY Legs

Parts of ME that hurt

MY BRAIN

My arms

My Legs

TOP VIEW

I am sure you are absolutely BUSTING to find out what happened next at Pony School, Diary, so I will write some more for you now, even though it makes my arms even hurtier.

When all our ponies were tacked up we took them back out into the horse yard. And then June told us to climb up onto their back parts so we could ride them around in a nice round ring.

I was just looking at how high up off the ground Patches' back part was and thinking maybe making horses my life wasn't such a good idea after all, when Zoe said, "Stop being such a Nervous Nella, Ella, it is easy-peasy getting onto a pony, I bet even my nonna could do it."

And then she gave me all these complicated instructions about what to do with your left hand and your right leg and your left foot and how to hold the ~~rains~~ reins properly, until I said, "Stop it, Zoe, you are making my head explode!"

ME and my Exploding HEAD!

Everything was hopelessly hopeless. How was I supposed to be an internationally famous bareback-riding circus star if I couldn't even climb up onto my pony?

I was just about ready to walk out the gates and go home. And then June tapped me on the shoulder and gave me a carrot.

Bleuchhh. I don't even *like* carrots.

Carrot

And then Zoe said, "It's not for you, silly, it's for your horse."

So I gave Patches the carrot and while he was MUNCH, MUNCH, CRUNCHING it I sneakily did all the foot and leg and hand things in the exact right order just like Zoe said to do, and then all of a sudden I was sitting up nice and straight on his back with my feet in the ~~syrups~~ stirrups!✳

HOW TO GET ONTO THE BACK PART OF A HORSE

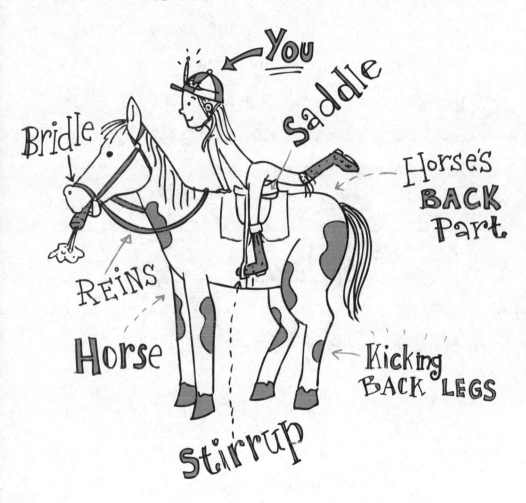

You

Saddle

Bridle

Horse's BACK Part.

Reins

Horse

Kicking BACK LEGS

Stirrup

* Zoe's Horsey Fact #7: Stirrups are the metal loops hanging off a saddle that you put your feet into so your legs don't fall off when you are riding. (Syrups are what you pour on top of pancakes and banana splits. Even people with REALLY tiny brains know that.)

And then I was ~~driving~~ riding him!

And I didn't even fall off!

It was aMAZing.

Zoe and I rode around and around in a circle
with the other Pony School girls.
All except one.

Guess who?

HINT: Her name
rhymes with "bleach."

She was still standing
next to her precious
palomino pony. Ha! Every
time she got close enough
to jump on, Blondie tossed
her golden head and moved
away.

PEACH

Peach was getting madder and madder, and Blondie was getting friskier and friskier. And then all of a sudden there was a flash of crashing hoofs and two sleek, shiny horses galloped over, right into the middle of our pony ring.

And guess who was riding them?

Lady Letitia and her snooty friend Lavinia.

Letitia climbed down from her horse, Misty.
Then she looked at Peach and said, "Having
trouble, sweetie? Watch and learn."

And then Letitia did all the climbing-up
things I just did, only better and more
~~elephantly~~ elegantly.

"See?" Letitia
said, climbing
down again. "Easy-
peasy. Now you
try, Peachy-Pie.
Don't worry. I'll hold
your sweel lillle
ponykins for you."

And then Letitia held Blondie's rein bits so Peach could climb up onto her back part.

Zoe and I exchanged another MEANINGFUL LOOK. Our heads were practically EXPLODING with important questions like:

Exchanging meaningful Looks

ZOE

ME

 How did Peach and Letitia know each other

 and why did they obviously hate each other so much?

And then you'll NEVER guess what happened next. Letitia did something really, really, REALLY mean to the power of 100 gazillion trillion to Peach.

She let go of Blondie's reins, just as Peach was jumping up to swing her leg over Blondie's back part.

Blondie moved away again.

And Peach fell off.

PHWOMPHH!

Peach

Right into the middle of a big, stinky, steaming pile of horse poop.

Big, stinky, STEAMING PILE OF HORSE POOP

Oops.

"Ha-ha-ha!" sniggered Letitia and Lavinia. Then they jumped back onto their perfect, sleek, shiny horses and cantered away.

Zoe and I were SHOCKED! Even Peach, who is the Queen of Mean, NEVER does stuff as nasty and mean as that.

Peach's face went all crumply. Then she glared at us in a glarey way and said, "What are YOU looking at?!?"

So we stopped looking at her and went back to riding our ponies instead.

All this writing is making me very exhausted, Diary. So I will stop now and get some sleep.

Tomorrow is going to be a REALLY big day. I hope I get Patches again.

XX

PS Olivia told me tonight Mom and Dad are getting me a REALLY BIG SURPRISE for my birthday next week. I wonder what it is?

I know!

IT'S A HORSE!

YES!!!!! ☺☺☺

Maybe they're going to get me Patches! That must be why they asked me the name of the horse I was riding!

DOUBLE YES!!!! ☺☺☺☺☺☺

Or maybe it ISN'T an ~~acksh~~ actual horse they're getting me at all. Maybe it's just a PICTURE of a horse.

Yes, that's probably it. ☹☹☹

But maybe . . .

A picture OF A HORSE

Thursday morning, before breakfast

Something really strange has happened to my legs.

I CAN'T WALK ON MY LEGS!!   HELP!

Thursday morning, twenty minutes later

Mom told me to stop screeching and have a really, really hot bath.

So I did. And now I can walk again. YAY!

Thursday night, in bed

Dearest Diary,

Today was THE BEST DAY EVER!

As soon as we arrived at Pony School I ran straight over to the horse yard to make sure I got Patches again. Whinny I gave his neck part a whole lot of patting pats and he did a big whinny. That must mean he was pleased to see me too!

Patches kept following me around everywhere trying to push his big nuzzly nose into my pocket. Zoe said he was looking for carrots. I didn't have any carrots, but I found an old bit of broccoli I hid in there once when Mom wasn't looking so I gave him that instead and he ate it all up just like Bob does, yum yum.

Then June came out of the horse shed and told everyone to tack up our ponies quickly because she was going to give us all a special riding lesson.

She showed us how to sit on our ponies nicely

with **OUR Heads UP**

And **our ELBOWS** in

and **our Backs** STRAIGHT

and **our HEELS** Down

and our toes UP

And then we had a lesson all about how to sit lightly on the saddle when we were doing trotting. June said we had to imagine there was a little baby bird on the saddle and to sit down very, very gently with our bottoms so we didn't squash it.

And then a girl called Jaime-Anna started
crying because she thought there really
were little baby birds getting squashed
under everyone's bottoms,
so we had to stop doing
that lesson and learn how
to hold the reins like they
were ice cream cones
instead.

Jaime-Anna

And then June told us to line up our horses
and ponies behind her in a big long line
because we were all going on a ~~trial~~ trail
ride through the lovely bushes.

It was aMAZing!

We did walking and trotting and we saw all my favorite nature things, like trees and flowers and birds, flitting around in the sunny sunshine. It was peaceful and lovely and I wanted it to go on FOREVER.

Patches is the BEST PONY in the history of ponies. He didn't keep stopping to eat grass, or speed up and bump into other ponies, or get all twitchy and tail-flicky and kicky, even when a gigantic lizard went for a walk across the trail right

Gigantic LiZARD

in front of him. He was PERFECTLY behaved. I wish we could go trail riding every day.

When I got home I wrote this poem about him.

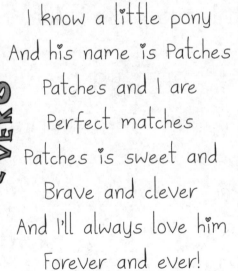

I know a little pony
And his name is Patches
Patches and I are
Perfect matches
Patches is sweet and
Brave and clever
And I'll always love him
Forever and ever!

When I looked out the window I saw a
wishing star in the sky. So I made this
wish:

Please, please, please can Mom and Dad
please buy Patches for me for my birthday.

I hope it comes true.

Good night, Diary.
Sweet dreams.
Ella xxx

Friday afternoon, straight after Pony School

You are NOT going to BELIEVE what happened at Pony School today!

We were playing this game called Musical Hoops. Musical Hoops is EXACTLY the same as Musical Chairs except you and your horse don't sit down in a chair, that would be silly. You race your horse over to the hoops and get it to put its two front legs inside one of the hoops like this:

TWO Front LEGS INSIDE THE HOOP

If your horse's legs aren't inside a hoop when the music stops, then you are O-U-T SPELLS **OUT.**

Everyone was playing, except for some of the older girls, like Abbey and Letitia and Lavinia, who were helping June blow up balloons for the Balloon Popping✳ game.

✳ Balloon Popping is a game the more experienced riders play. It looks like even MORE fun than Musical Hoops. You have to pop balloons with a stick while you ride past them on your horse.

Balloon POPPING Game

POP

We were all having lots of fabulous fun.
And then . . .

Da da da DUMMM....

Letitia accidentally on purpose popped the balloon she was blowing up, just as Peach was riding past on Blondie. And Blondie got spooked.**

SPOOKED HORSE!

Ghost

** Zoe's Horsey Fact #8: If a horse is spooked it means something gave it a fright, like an unexpected loud noise or a hot air balloon whooshing past. It does NOT mean it saw a ghost.

First Blondie's ears went *Snorting Whinny* all flat. Then her tail went all twitchy. And then she stood up on her back legs and did a big snorting whinny, just like Misty did when I spooked *her*.

And then she took off. (With Peach still on her back part.)

They went across the Musical Hoops field and around the back of the horse shed and over the horse paddock and up to the fence.

The Good News

Wheeeee!

BLONDiE STOPPED

Blondie stopped.

The Bad News

Peach didn't stop. She went "WHEEEEEEEE!"
right over the top of Blondie's head.

The Worse News

There was a muddy ditch on the other side
of the fence.

The Better News

Peach landed right in the middle of the muddy ditch so she didn't break any bones.

The ~~Worst~~ Better News
(I can't decide)

Her beautiful stylish white and gold everything riding outfit was now ugly and smelly black and black everything. And so was her face.

Zoe and I were SHOCKED! How DARE Letitia do that to Peach? (Even if she is a big meanie herself, she used to be my BFF, and anyway, NOBODY deserves to be treated LIKE THAT!)

So we IMMEDIATELY dashed over on our plucky ponies like heroic heroines to help Peach climb up out of the muddy ditch. But she just gave us an evil look and said, "I'm fine, thank you very much, now go away."

To The Rescue

And then Letitia turned up on HER horse.

This is what happened next.

Letitia (staring down at Peach): That was
for my mom.
Peach (eyes like daggers): You are SO dead.
Letitia (eyes like bigger daggers): Says
who?
Peach (icily): Says me. And MY mom.
Letitia (icily): Drop in a hole, Peach. Oh, wait,
you already did! Ha-ha-ha.

Then she galloped
away into the
setting sun.

Peach and Letitia
are ~~WIRED~~ ~~WIERD~~
WEIRD.

Friday night, just before lights-out

Dearest Diary,

I can't stop thinking about what happened today with Peach and Letitia. Letitia is SO MEAN! WAY meaner than Peach. She must be feeling AWFUL. Maybe I should start being her friend again?

I'm going to ask Zoe what she thinks when we're at Pony School tomorrow.

Good night, Diary.

Sweet dreams. (YOU KNOW what I'll be dreaming about. ☺)
Ella xoxo

Saturday evening, after Pony School

Dear Diary,

I am in DESPERATE DESPAIR. So desperate I will probably die a sad and tragic death and/or wither away to nothing.

Here's what happened.

As soon as Zoe and I arrived at Pony School I ran over to the horse yard to get Patches but he wasn't there!

I looked in the horse shed and the tack room and called his name and even did some super-shrill whinnies, in case he was way up at the other end of the horse paddock, so he would know I was happy and excited to see him and come ~~galumphing~~ galloping across the fields to nuzzle my face with his velvety nose.

Whinny

Whinny

And then June saw me looking
and said she was sorry but
someone else had already
taken Patches for today. In
fact, she had reserved him for
the whole rest of the school
vacation but it was OK, I
could have Blondie instead.

Blondie???

?!

BLondie?!!

And then Peach trotted past me on Patches
with this ginormous sneery smirk all over
her smirky sneery face.

How DARE she?!?

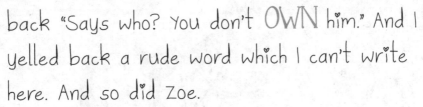

So I yelled, "Hey,
that's MY horse!"
and Peach yelled
back "Says who? You don't OWN him." And I
yelled back a rude word which I can't write
here. And so did Zoe.

And then Peach called out, "Tootles!" and gave
us both a little wave as she rode off into
the distance.

Waaaaahhh! She makes me SO MAD!

That is absolutely the last time I ever feel sorry for, or offer to help, Precious Princess Peach Parker do anything again. Ever.

Saturday night, very, very late

I am trying to be brave, but I am inconsolable.*

inconsolaBLe

* Inconsolable means nobody can cheer you up, not even if they told you that you and your family and all your BFFs were going to

live on a horse ranch
with unlimited horses
to ride and/or ice
cream to eat forever
and ever.

What if Peach likes Patches so much she tries
to persuade her mom to buy him for her, only
her mom says no? So then she runs away to
the circus with him and I never see him or get
to ride him ever again???

Sunday night, before lights-out

My dearest Diary,

It was very rainy all day. So rainy that
Mom said it was too wet to go to Pony
School, so Dad took me, and Zoe and Olivia
to the movies and my favorite ice cream
parlor as a special early birthday treat
instead.

when we got home, Max was pretending the kitchen broom was a horsey and was riding it around and around the family room.

And Mom had one of those guilty looks on her face that she always gets when she is planning a special secret surprise for you and she doesn't want you to know what it is.

And of course I guessed what the secret was straightaway!

Patches probably wouldn't let Peach ride
him because he was pining for me, so she
wouldn't want him anymore.

Which meant Mom and Dad could buy him
for my birthday tomorrow after all! Mom
probably spent the WHOLE TIME we were
out organizing it all with the Pony School.

I CAN'T WAIT until tomorrow!

Monday morning, after breakfast but before Pony School

Dearest Diary,

It's my birthday!

Dad brought me my favorite breakfast in bed.

Pancakes ⸮ ⸮ ⸮ with ice cream AND MAPLE ~~Stirrup~~ SYRUP

just Kidding! JOKE HaHa

And then everyone gave me my presents.
Here's what I got:

Notebook

Model HORSE

RIDING BOOTS

Horse HEAD CANDLE

Jewelry BOX

Joddies

But the BEST present of all is secretly
waiting for me at Pony School. He-he.

I'll be back soon to tell you ALL ABOUT IT!

E xx

Monday night, in bed, totally exhausted

Dearest, darlingest Diary,

I was so excited on the way to Pony School about my secret surprise that I couldn't sit still! I kept thinking about all the things Patches and I could do together once he was my horse for always and forever. He would be like my own special Star.

But guess what? When we got to Pony School there was nobody there. Not even June, and she's ALWAYS there. And it was really, really quiet. It was like an alien spacecraft had landed in the horse paddock and sucked all the riders and ponies and horses into a black hole.

And then the door
of the horse shed
opened up a teeny
tiny bit and Jaime-
Anna and Abbey
trotted out and
whispered, "Quick,
June needs to see
you URGENTLY!"

And I thought, Yes!
My wish is finally
going to come true!

So I went into the horse shed but instead of seeing Patches with a big blue birthday ribbon around him, I saw my family and lots of the girls from Vacation Club and even some of my friends from school, like Georgia and Chloe and Cordelia.

And then they all called out "Surprise!" and threw streamers and glitterized cutout paper horseshoes at me.

And there was a big table with
cute little cupcakes that had
horseshoes on them and napkins
and paper plates and drinking cups
with horsey designs and right in
the middle was a beautiful horsey
birthday cake that looked like this:

Zow-ee! Mom and Nanna Kate must have spent the WHOLE DAY in here yesterday setting all this up.

And even though I was really, really happy about the surprise birthday party my lovely family and friends made for me, I was a little bit sad too, because it meant Patches wasn't going to be mine for always and forever after all.

But then somebody turned the music up really loud and everybody danced and we played funny games like Pin the Tail

Pin THE Tail ON the Horse

TaiL

on the Horse and Musical
Horsey Statues, and then we
tacked up our horses and
played more games outside
like Balloon Popping and
Musical Hoops and it turned
out to be the BEST
BIRTHDAY EVER.

Balloon POPPING
Game

POP

Catch you later, Diary!
Lots of love,
Ella

PS (two days later)

Guess what?!

After Peach came home on the weekend with all her beautiful white clothes covered in icky sticky mud, her mom said she wasn't ~~aloud~~ allowed to go back to Pony School EVER AGAIN.

Which means I can ride Patches whenever I want to! YES!!!!

PPS (one week later)

And guess what else?

I found out why Princess Peach and Lady Letitia hate each other so much. Their moms are TWIN SISTERS, which means Letitia and Peach are COUSINS! No wonder I thought they looked just like evil sisters!

EVIL SISTERS ??!

And when their moms were our age, about 900 years ago, they were both really, really good horse-riding show jumpers. And one day they were both competing for the same trophy and Peach's mom spooked Letitia's mom's horse just as she was about to do her ride for the trophy, and Letitia's mom fell off into a (dried-up) muddy ditch and broke her arm in three places! And then Peach's mom won.

Zow-ee. That explains EVERYTHING!

CYA!
Love, Ella

Diaries

Read them all!